# EILEEN CHRISTELOW'S
# FIVE Little
# MONKEYS
# SUPER STICKER
# ACTIVITY BOOK

Houghton Mifflin Harcourt
Boston   New York   2009

# FIVE LITTLE MONKEYS JUMPING ON THE BED

## Draw a picture of yourself jumping with the monkeys!

## TIME TO GET DRESSED!

What is the weather like outside? Draw it in!

What should this little monkey wear today? Draw an outfit for him.

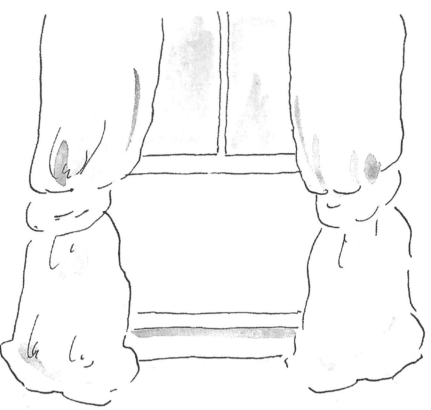

# DRAW IT IN!

It's easy to get sleepy after a yummy picnic. What is Mama dreaming about?

**IT'S SMOKY IN HERE!**

**What are the monkeys baking in the oven?**

# THE MONKEYS' TOYS ARE EVERYWHERE! MAMA WANTS THEM CLEANED UP.

How many round toys do you see? _____

How many trucks can you count? _____

How many monkeys can you find? _____

How many pairs of glasses do you see? _____

How many marbles can you count? _____

How many hats can you find? _____

# LET'S GO!

Can you help the monkeys
find their way home?

**START**

**FINISH**

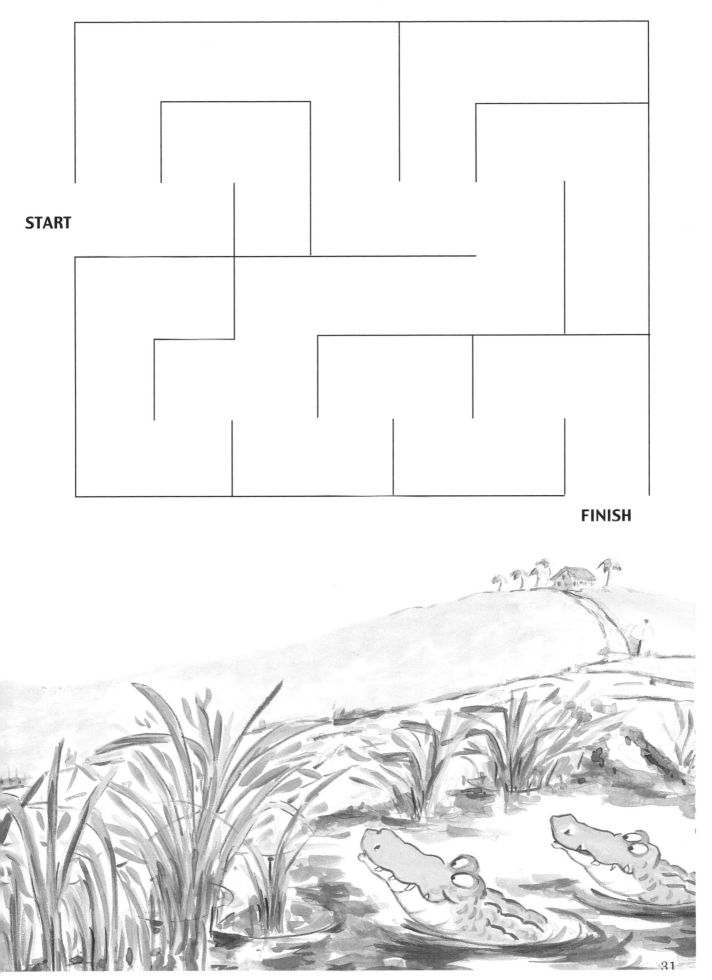

# LEARN HOW TO DRAW A MONKEY!

## Follow these steps and draw your very own monkey:

**1** First draw a circle with two dots.

**2** Add two big eyes.

**3** This monkey needs fur.

**4** And two ears!

**5** And what about a mouth? Is he happy?

**6** Or is your monkey sad?

**7** And don't forget the eyebrows! They show how your monkey feels, too.

**8** Here are some silly monkeys making funny faces. Look at their eyes, mouths, and eyebrows.

**9** Here are some more monkeys. Can you give them silly faces?

# NOW YOUR MONKEY NEEDS A BODY!

You know how to draw a head!

Another arm

Draw an arm and a hand with 5 fingers.

Belly button

Squiggly tummy fur

Add squiggles here and there for fur.

2 legs

2 feet with 5 toes each

# DRAW YOUR OWN MONKEY HERE!

# TIME TO DRAW!

## Can you draw another little monkey?

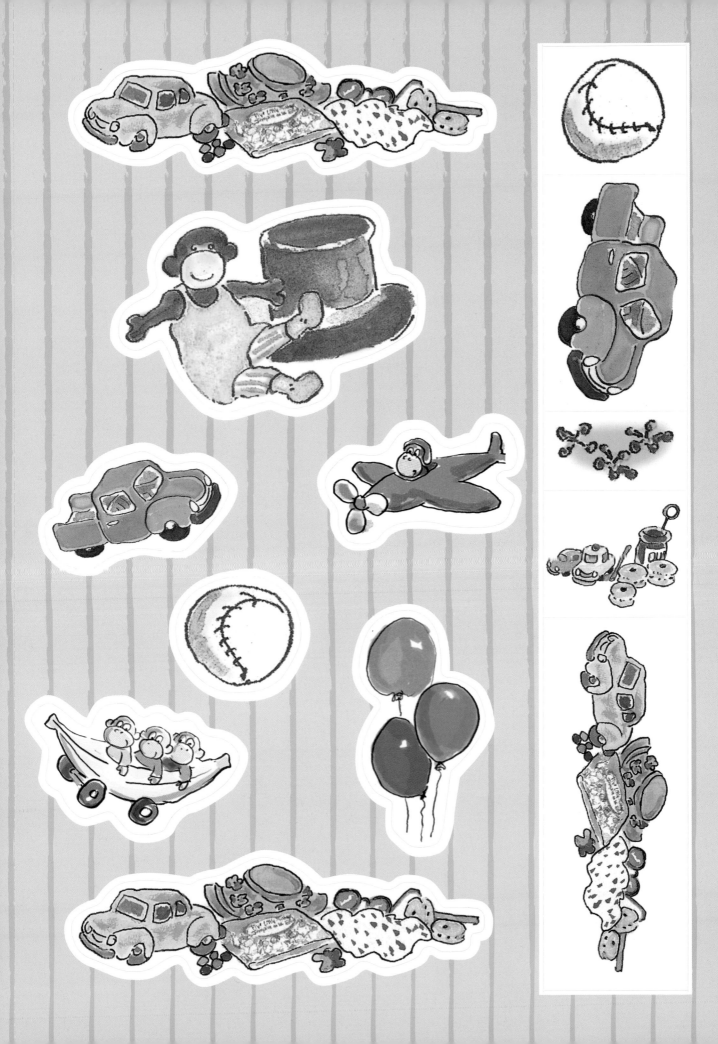

# TIC-TAC-TOE!

## Can you get three *x*'s or *o*'s in a row before your opponent can?

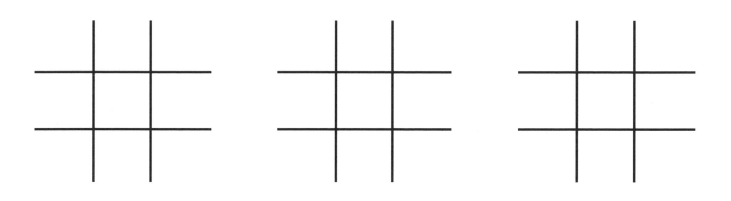

# WHAT IS MAMA THINKING ABOUT?

## Draw it in!

# THE MONKEYS ARE BUSY BUILDERS!

## What are they making?
## Can you draw it?

# TRAVELING IN STYLE!

## Can you help the monkeys decorate these cars? You can use your crayons or stickers!

# WHAT DO THE MONKEYS HAVE TO EAT FOR THEIR PICNIC LUNCH?

## Draw it in, or use your stickers!

# MAMA'S CALLING! CAN YOU HELP THIS LITTLE MONKEY FIND HER WAY HOME?

**Choose a path for her, but make sure she doesn't step on any bushes!**

# THE MONKEYS ARE HIDING!

## Can you help Lulu find them?

# WHAT A DIRTY CAR!

Can you help the monkeys wash or decorate it before they sell it? Use your stickers!

# TIME TO DRAW!

## What do the monkeys see?

# IT'S SNACKTIME!

How many berries do you see?
What kind of weather do the monkeys
have for berry picking? Draw it in!

# MATCH THE MONKEY!

Uh–oh! Some of these monkeys have gotten hurt. Can you match the hurt monkey to the monkey in the bed?

1   2   3   4   5

1 _____

2 _____

3 _____

4 _____

5 _____

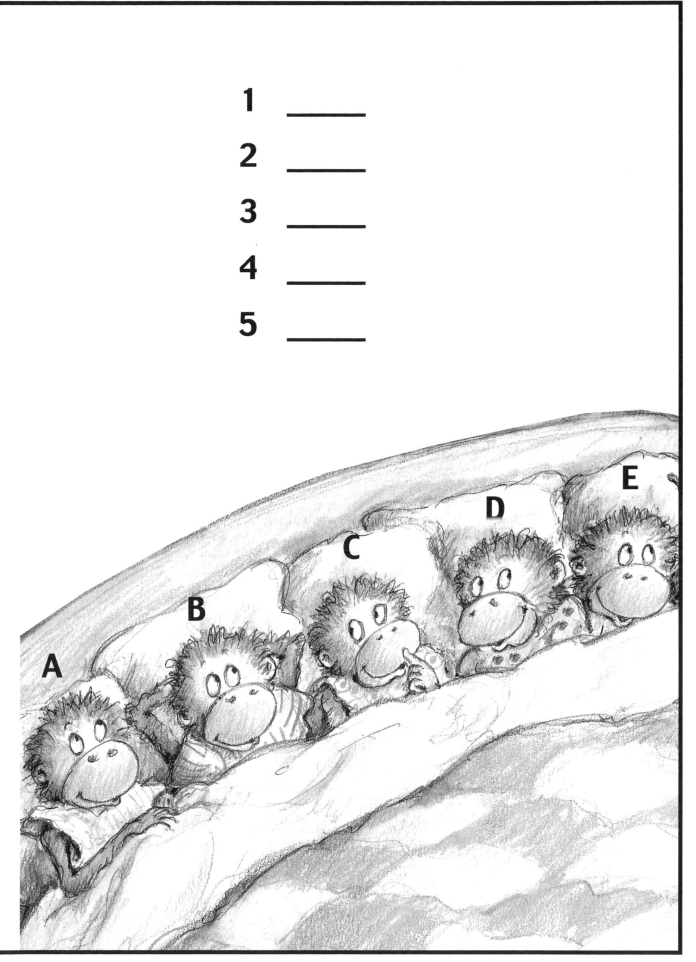

# WRITE IT IN!

## What did the doctor say about those hurt monkeys?

_ _ _ _ _ _ _ _ _ _ _ _ _ _ _ _ _ _ _ _ _ _ _ _ _ _

_ _ _ _ _ _ _ _ _ _ _ _ _ _ _ _ _ _ _ _ _ _ _ _ _ _

_ _ _ _ _ _ _ _ _ _ _ _ _ _ _ _ _ _ _ _ _ _ _ _ _ _

# DRAW IT IN!

## What, or who, is Lulu looking for?

# WHAT TIME IS IT?

## What time do you put on your pajamas at night?

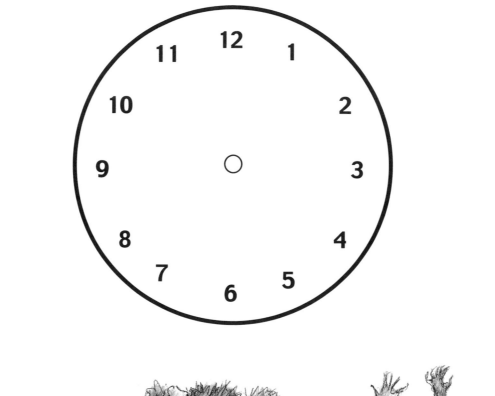

# What time do you brush your teeth in the morning?

# THE MONKEYS NEED TO GET TO SHORE!

## Can you draw a way for them to reach Mama safely?

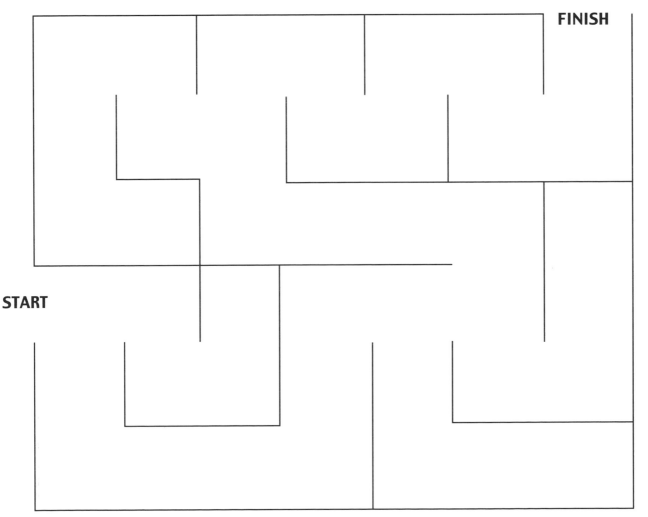

FINISH

START

# FIND THEM ALL!

How many  cars can you count?

How many  cars can you count?

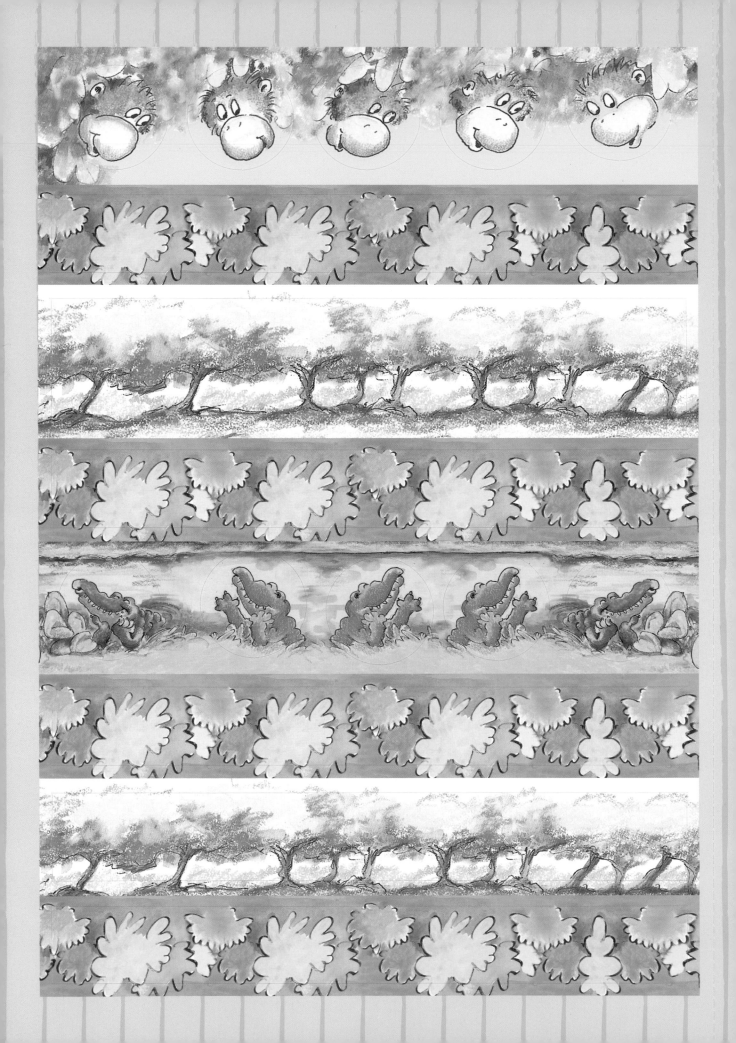

# INVENT YOUR OWN CAR!

## Draw it in!

# SHHH! THE MONKEYS ARE BEING VERY QUIET . . .

## Why are they tiptoeing? Write it in!

_ _ _ _ _ _ _ _ _ _ _ _ _ _ _ _ _ _ _ _ _ _

_ _ _ _ _ _ _ _ _ _ _ _ _ _ _ _ _ _ _ _ _ _

_ _ _ _ _ _ _ _ _ _ _ _ _ _ _ _ _ _ _ _ _ _

_ _ _ _ _ _ _ _ _ _ _ _ _ _ _ _ _ _ _ _ _ _

# THIS LITTLE MONKEY CAN CARRY A LOT!

## How many more things can you add to her load?

# UH-OH! SOME OF THESE LITTLE MONKEYS HAVE GOTTEN HURT.

Can you circle the monkeys that need to visit the doctor? Use your stickers to make sure those bandages hold!

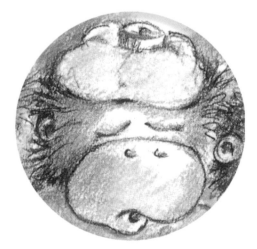

# THESE CROCODILES LOVE THEIR SWAMP HOME . . .

**What do you think the rest of the swamp looks like? Who else might live there? Draw it in!**

# TIME TO DRAW!

## Who is in the monkeys' picture frame?

Som of t  s bandag s  av  to b  d corat d!

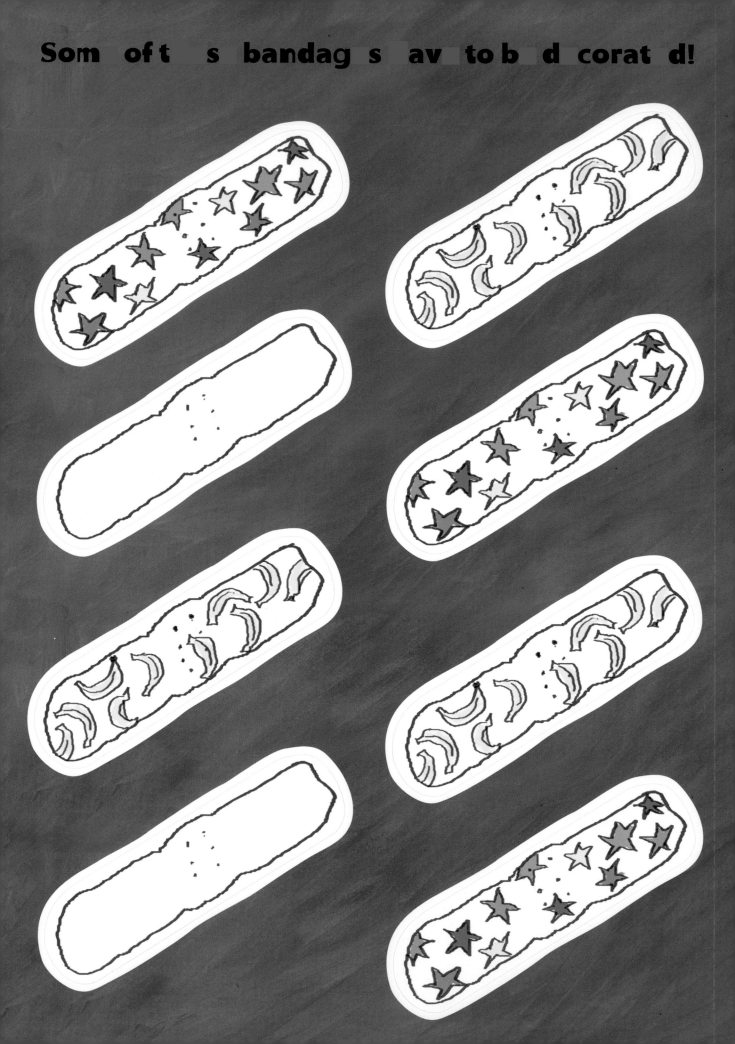

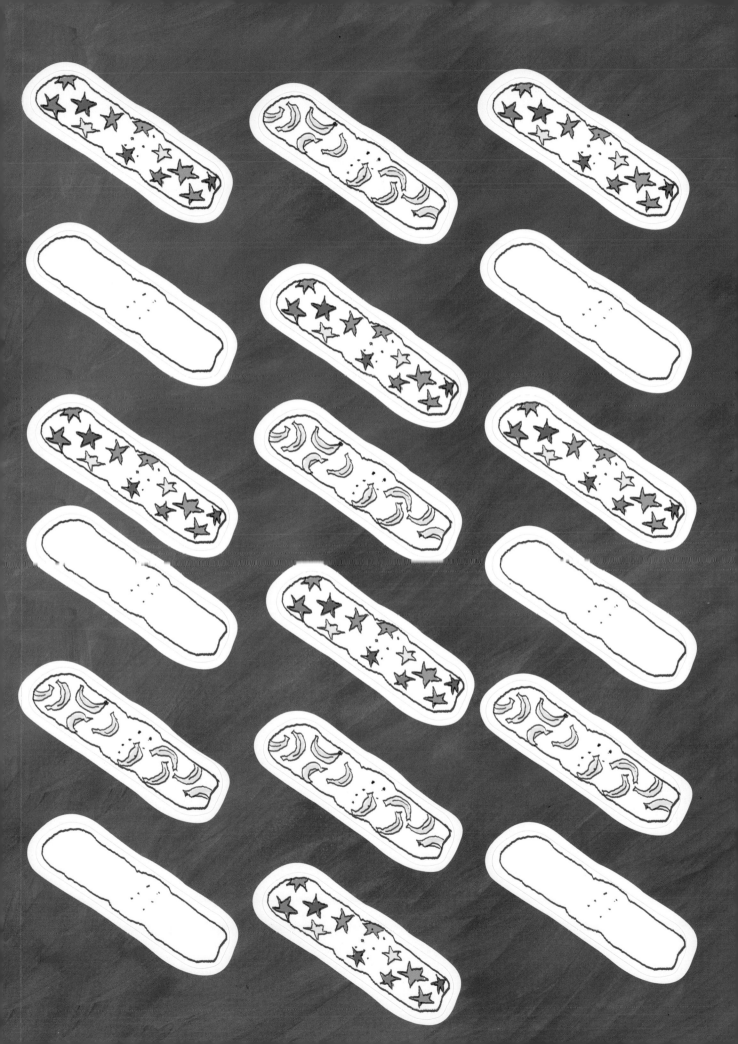

# MONKEYING AROUND!

## What are the monkeys looking at in the water below? Draw it in! Why are they hiding in the tree?

# THE MONKEYS ARE GOING ON A TRIP!

## What should they pack in their suitcase?

# Draw it in!

# GOOD MORNING!

## The monkeys just woke up!
## What's going on outside?

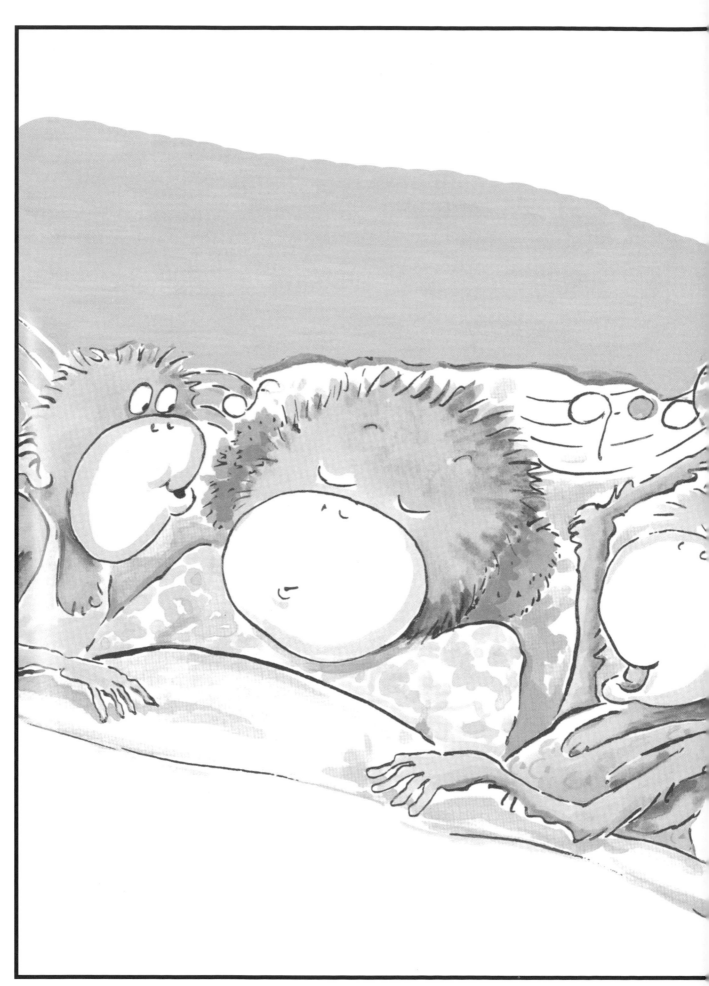

# IT'S MAMA'S BIRTHDAY!

**What do you think these monkeys are singing to wake Mama up? Can you draw a picture of her birthday cake?**

# JUST FOR YOU!

This little monkey is carrying a sign just for you! Can you write your name in it?

# TIME TO GO SHOPPING!

## What will the monkeys buy at the store?

# HMM . . . THERE'S A PATTERN!

## What comes next in each row?

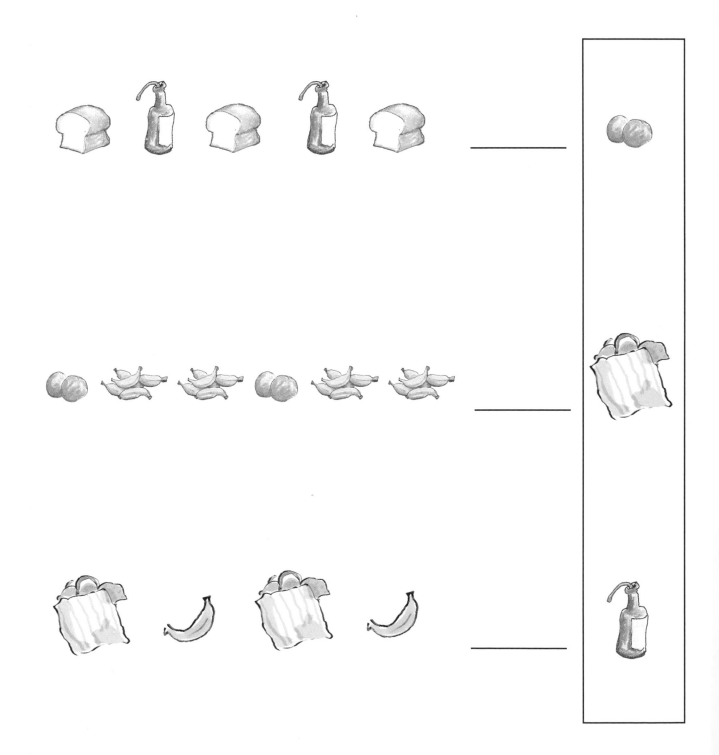

# THESE CARS ARE NOT QUITE THE SAME!

## Can you find at least four differences?

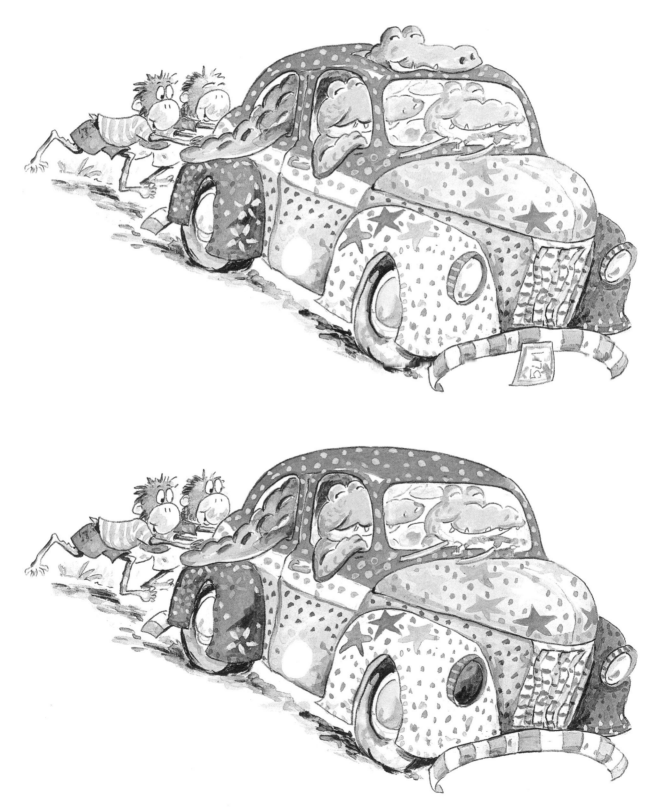

# TIME TO ADD!

## Write the number of the objects and add them up!

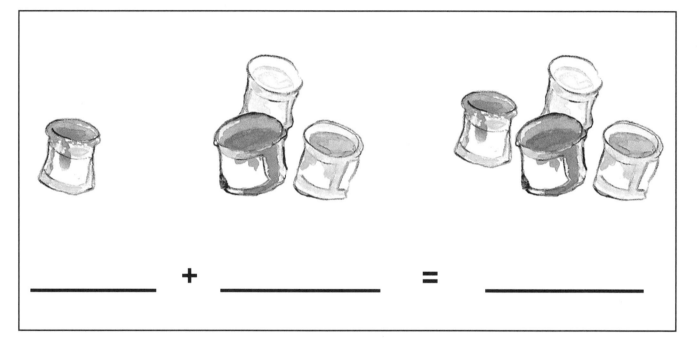

_____ + _____ = _____

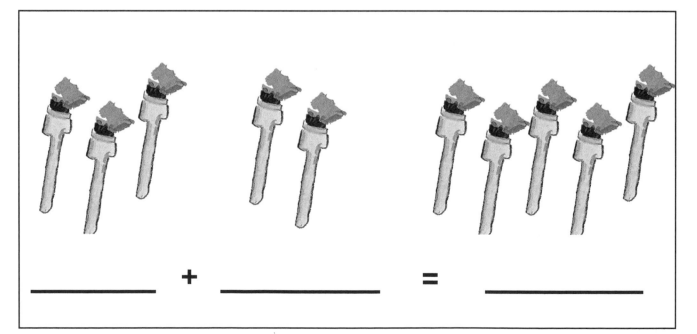

_____ + _____ = _____

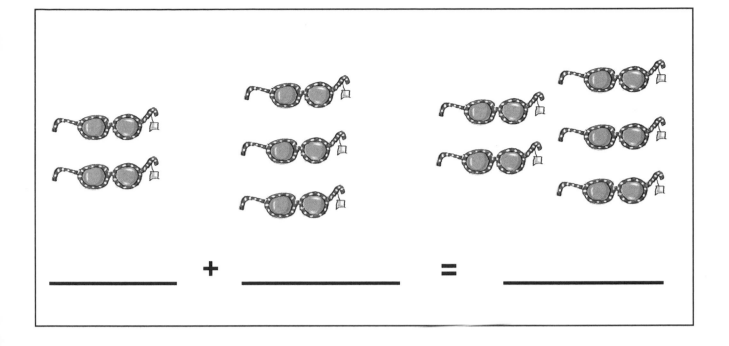

_____ + _____ = _____

_____ + _____ = _____

# STICKER FUN!

The monkeys are looking a little drab. That's probably why they are going shopping. Jazz them up by coloring or using your clothing stickers!

Copyright © 2009 by
Houghton Mifflin Harcourt Publishing Company
Art copyright © 2009 by Eileen Christelow
Activities created by Kelly Loughman
Designed by Carol Chu

Hougton Mifflin Harcourt
www.hmhbooks.com

ISBN-13: 978-0-547-14419-1

Manufactured in China
LEO 10 9 8 7 6 5 4 3 2 1

For more information about the author of the Five Little Monkeys series of books,
visit her website at www.christelow.com.

4. If you and someone else call out "SNAP!" together, the person with his hand at the bottom of the pile is the one who gets the cards — as long as that person remembered to touch his forehead first!

5. If you call out "SNAP!" by mistake you must place three of your unturned cards in the center of the table.

6. The player who SNAPs all of the cards is the winner!

# How to play Snap:

For 2 to 4 players

1. Deal all 36 cards. Place your stack of cards face-down on the table in front of you.

2. On your turn, take the top card of your pack and place it face-up in a new pile in the center of the table.

3. If two cards in a row are the same, touch your forehead, yell "SNAP!" and place your hand on the pile. Take all the cards in the pile. Add these cards to the bottom of your main stack of cards (face-down).

SNAP!

SNAP!

SNAP!

SNAP!

SNAP!

SNAP!

SNAP!

# FINGER PUPPET FUN!

## Punch out and play with your very own mischievous monkeys.